Dr. Jekyll and Mr. Hyde

By Robert Louis Stevenson

Adapted by Kate McMullan
Illustrated by Paul Van Munching

BULLSEYE CHILLERS™

RANDOM HOUSE 🏠 **NEW YORK**

For J.B.

A BULLSEYE BOOK PUBLISHED BY RANDOM HOUSE, INC.

Text copyright © 1984 by Kate McMullan. Illustrations copyright © 1984 by Random House, Inc. Cover illustration copyright © 1994 by Steve Brennan. All rights reserved under International and Pan-American Copyright Conventions. Published in the United States by Random House, Inc., New York, and simultaneously in Canada by Random House of Canada Limited, Toronto. Originally published by Random House, Inc., in 1984.

Library of Congress Cataloging-in-Publication Data:
McMullan, Kate.   Dr. Jekyll and Mr. Hyde.   (Step-up classic chillers)
Adaptation of: The strange case of Dr. Jekyll and Mr. Hyde.
SUMMARY: A kind and well-respected doctor can turn himself into a murderous madman by taking a secret drug he's created.
[1. Horror stories]   I. Van Munching, Paul, ill.   II. Stevenson, Robert Louis, 1850–1894. Strange case of Dr. Jekyll and Mr. Hyde.
III. Title.   IV. Series.   PZ7.M47879Dr   1988   [Fic]   87-23542
ISBN: 0-394-86365-8 (pbk.)

First Random House Bullseye Books edition: 1994

Manufactured in the United States of America   20 19 18 17 16 15

DR. JEKYLL AND MR. HYDE

No one has ever suffered as I have. No one! This is the last time that I, Dr. Henry Jekyll, can think my own thoughts. Or see my own face in the mirror.

Soon I will turn into Edward Hyde again. And that will be the end of Henry Jekyll. Forever!

So I must hurry. I must write down my story while I still can. I do not know if anyone will ever read it. What if Hyde finds my writing? He will tear it to bits. But I must tell my story. And so, let me begin.

Chapter 1

I remember everything about the night I first took the drug. The magic drug that changed me into Edward Hyde.

I was a well-known doctor. One of the best in London. Many sick people came to me. And I helped them all.

On this day I was just showing a young woman to the door. In her arms she held a baby. She looked up at me with tears in her eyes.

"Doctor," she began, "I thank you. With all my heart. I was so afraid that my baby was not going to live. If only . . . if only I had some money. . . ."

"Do not think about paying me," I told her. "Seeing your little girl smile is enough for me. See that she gets a lot of rest now."

"Thank you," she said again. And she went out.

As I closed the door I noticed my butler, Poole. He had been watching me.

"You look tired, sir," he said. "You should get some rest too."

I looked at the clock. It *had* been a long day.

"You are right, Poole," I said. "You may get dinner ready now. I need to eat. I have a long night before me. In my lab."

"Yes, sir," said Poole. He turned to go. But he turned back again.

"You do so much good, sir," he said. "So much good."

With that, he left.

I shook my head.

"If he only knew," I thought. "If he only knew that there is another side to me. A side that I hide. A side that is not good at all!"

I had to smile. Poole probably thought that I was working in my lab on some new medicine. Something that would help people. But that was far, far from the truth.

That night, after dinner, I went to my lab. A fire was burning in the fireplace. It threw shadows of strange shapes against the wall. I could see the blood-red liquid in a glass by the table. My magic drug! It was almost ready. Next to the glass was a large pile of white powder. I had bought all I could from a nearby drugstore.

It was the only thing I still needed for my experiment.

No one had ever made a drug like this before! It was going to change me completely. I stared at it for a long time. There it was! A drug so strong that it could separate the good side of me and the bad side of me into two people! Think of it! The good side could go on working to make the world a better place. Never bothered by any wicked thoughts. While the other side could be as bad as it liked. And there would be no good side to make it feel ashamed.

I sat back. I remembered all the people who had made fun of me! Like my old friend Dr. Lanyon. Why, he had laughed out loud when I told him that each person is not really one person, but two. I remembered this. And I smiled.

Slowly I poured the white powder into the glass. The red liquid smoked and boiled. There! It was finished. I knew that I might die if I took the drug. But I had to know if it worked!

I lifted the blood-red liquid to my lips and drank it down.

I let out a cry! The pain! It burned through me like fire! My bones felt as if they were being broken to bits. I shook like a flag in the wind. I was sick. So sick I wanted to die. But suddenly the pain stopped. I began to feel something new. I felt younger and lighter. I felt that I could do anything.

I turned and looked into the mirror. I saw before me a brand-new person. I was a much smaller man than I had been. My coat sleeves hung way past the tips of my fingers. I looked like a young boy in his father's clothes. I was smaller, yes, and younger. And very strange looking. The hair on my head was thick and wild. My eyes were small. Small and mean. My nose was flat and my teeth were sharp and crooked. I knew I was ugly. But I

liked this new face. This, too, was me. The evil side of me. This was the part of me that, all these years, I felt I had to hide. And so I gave this new me a new name. Mr. Hyde. Mr. Edward Hyde.

I walked around the room. Even my walk was different. Henry Jekyll was a big, tall man. He had a slow, heavy step. Edward Hyde's step was quicker, lighter. It had a strange swing to it too.

My new voice was the next thing I tried. It was a low, rough whisper.

I sat down at my desk and took out paper and pen. I was surprised to find that my handwriting was the one thing about me that had not changed.

And so I spent the evening. I got to know everything I could about

Edward Hyde. At last I saw that morning was coming. Poole would be up soon. He would be waiting to make breakfast for Henry Jekyll. But I did not yet know if the magic drug would bring back the good doctor.

Quickly I poured more white powder into another glass of the red liquid. Once again I drank the smoking drink. And once again I felt the shaking. The pain! The breaking of my bones!

When, at last, the pain stopped, I looked into the mirror. There, looking back at me, was the kind face of Dr. Henry Jekyll.

Chapter 2

The next day I saw many sick people. But my mind was not on them. I was thinking about Edward Hyde. He was real! And so I had to make a place for him in the world.

In the afternoon I closed my office. I went out to the shops. I was looking for clothes in a small size. Edward Hyde's size. As I shopped I wondered. Why was Hyde so much smaller and younger than Jekyll? And why wasn't Hyde as strong as Jekyll? Then it came to me. Most of my life, I had been very good. I had not used my bad side much. So it was not as big or as strong as my good side.

At the shops I picked out fine clothes. Evening clothes. For the night was to belong to Edward Hyde.

When I came back home, I called Poole and Amanda, my maid, into the living room. "A man named Edward Hyde," I began, "will visit this house often. I have given him the door keys. He is free to come and go as he likes. Treat him well. Do all that he wishes. Do you understand?"

"Yes, sir," they both said.

As Poole left the room, I saw his face. He looked puzzled. I had always lived alone. He did not understand this change.

That night I asked my lawyer, Mr. Utterson, to visit me. Poole showed him into my sitting room.

"Hello, Jekyll," said Utterson. "I am glad to see you. It has been a long time, you know. You are so busy with your work."

"Yes, Utterson," I replied. "I have so much to do. Please. Take a seat. I have asked you here to talk about my will."

"Your will?" asked Utterson. "I believe it is in order."

"There are some changes I want to make," I told Utterson. I handed him a sheet of paper. "Here is my new will."

Utterson looked over the new will.

"If you die," he said slowly as he read the paper, "you wish to leave everything to your friend Edward Hyde." He looked up at me. "But, Jekyll! What can be the meaning of this? It also says here that if you are missing for three months, Edward Hyde is to get everything you own!"

"Yes, Utterson," I said.

"But this is madness!" exclaimed Utterson. "Madness! Who is this Hyde? I have never even heard you speak of him before."

"No. You have not," I answered. "He is a new friend. A very close friend. A young man who means a lot to me."

"But, Henry!" said Utterson. "This

is so sudden! Is there some problem?
Is this Hyde making you change your
will?"

"Not at all," I said.

Utterson was quiet. Then he said,
"As your lawyer, I cannot let you do
this."

"But you have to," I replied.

"Very well," said Utterson. "I will
take what you have written. And if
something happens to you, I will see
that your will is carried out. But I
will never approve of such a thing."

Utterson left quickly. I watched him
go. He was a good friend. And a good
lawyer too. Of course, he was right.
It was madness! A madness that excited me as nothing had ever done
before!

When Utterson was gone, I went

to my lab. I got out the clothes I had bought that day. And then I made the drug. I swallowed every drop. The shaking came on me as before. It was horrible. Horrible! But at last it stopped. And again I had turned into Edward Hyde.

I wasted no time. I changed into my new clothes. I took my cane. Then I headed out the back door of the lab and into the street.

Oh! How free I felt! I walked down streets I had walked all my life. I saw people I knew well. But they had no idea who I was! The good doctor had been left behind.

At a corner I spotted a horse and carriage. Quickly I climbed in.

"Take me to Soho!" I shouted to the driver. "And hurry up about it!"

"Yes, sir!" answered the driver. He looked at me strangely. I saw that he had no liking for me.

The carriage started rolling. Soho was a dark and dangerous part of London that I loved well. I had gone there before a few times as Henry Jekyll. But I was always afraid that someone would know me. But now that fear was gone. I was Edward Hyde. Going out for a night on the town.

The carriage stopped.

"Here we are, sir," the driver said. "Soho."

I jumped out of the carriage. I threw a few coins onto the ground and laughed. "You want your money? Then dig for it!" And off I went into the night.

What a time I had! I drank and drank. I got into fights. I could see in people's eyes that they were afraid of me. They backed off when I came near. This just excited me! I laughed in their scared faces.

At last, places in Soho began to close. It was almost morning. But I was not ready to go to Jekyll's home. Not yet.

A sign on a street caught my eye. ROOMS FOR RENT. I thought to myself, "Hyde needs a home. Perhaps this might be the place."

I rang the bell under the sign. An old woman popped her head out a window above me.

"What do you want?" she yelled.

"The rooms!" I called. "Let me see them!"

"At this hour?" she exclaimed. "Good people are still in their beds so early in the morning."

"Now!" I shouted. "And be quick about it!"

In a minute the old woman came to the door. She looked me over. And then she said, "Yes. These rooms will do for the likes of you."

She led me up the steps and opened a door. The rooms were small. The windows were dirty. But what did I care? I only wanted a place for Edward Hyde to sleep when he did not want to stay at Jekyll's home.

"I'll take the rooms," I said.

I gave the old woman the first month's rent. She grabbed the money.

"Your name, sir?" she asked. "I don't ask more of you than that."

"The name is Hyde," I said. "Edward Hyde."

I put the keys in my pocket. Then I turned and started back to Jekyll's house. It was morning now. London was waking up. Even though I had not slept, I wasn't tired. I felt good. I walked fast. I was thinking about the night I had just had. All of a sudden a child came around the corner.

"Out of my way!" I yelled. I knocked into the child and down she fell. Did I stop then? No! I just walked right over her. The child screamed.

I would have kept going. But I felt a strong hand grab me. I turned and saw an angry face.

"What is the meaning of this?" a tall man said. He held me tight. "Have you no feelings? You hurt this child!

And yet you walk on!"

The man looked at me. Anger and hate showed in his face. I knew that face from somewhere. Who was this man? I could not remember.

A crowd was growing around us. The child's father was there. He was holding the little girl in his arms. Someone sent for a doctor. The doctor came and bent over the crying

child. Then the doctor looked at me and said, "Who are you, sir?"

"Edward Hyde is the name," I said.

"And what are you going to do to help this poor child?" he asked.

"Nothing," I said.

"Nothing?" said the tall man. "That policeman over there will know how to take care of you!"

"That's right. Jail is the place for you!" shouted the child's father.

Jail! The very thought of it froze me! I could not stand that.

"I see you mean to make trouble for me," I said. "Never mind the police. What do you want? Name your price."

"One hundred pounds,"* said the

*One hundred pounds is about $150.

tall man. "One hundred pounds for the child's family!"

By now, all the people standing around the hurt child were angry. Some tried to hit and scratch me. They wanted to kill me! The three men pulled me away from the crowd.

"Of course, I don't have that kind of money with me," I explained when I was safe. What could I do? I could think of only one thing. "I can get you a check," I said.

The three men followed me to the door of my lab. I went in, shutting the door in their faces. I went straight to Henry Jekyll's desk and took out his checkbook. I wrote out a check. I smiled as I signed it in Henry Jekyll's name.

In a few minutes I came out again.

I handed them the check.

The tall man looked at it hard. "But . . . can it be true?" he said. "This check is signed by Dr. Henry Jekyll! My cousin, Gabriel Utterson, is his lawyer. Jekyll is a fine man. He would never write a check for the likes of you!"

So this man was Utterson's cousin! Of course! I had seen them walking together in the park many times.

"The check is good," I said. "I will come with you to the bank. You will see."

And so we all went off to the bank. When it opened, we went in. Soon they had the money. The looks on their faces! I can see them still! They did not know what to think.

I laughed as I walked away and left them standing there. Edward Hyde could do just as he pleased in this world! And Henry Jekyll would have to pay for it!

Chapter 3

That night I, Henry Jekyll, sat over my dinner. The bell rang. Poole came into the room.

"Mr. Utterson is here to see you, sir," he said.

"Show him in," I said.

I stood up to meet my old friend. I held out my hand to him. But he hardly saw me. He had a worried look on his face.

"Henry!" he said. "I must speak to you. My cousin Richard Enfield came to see me this morning. He told me of a horrible thing that happened. And it was all caused by your new friend, Mr. Hyde."

I nodded. "I understand that he had a little problem this morning," I said.

"Little problem!" Utterson exclaimed. "Those are not the words for what happened! Enfield saw it with his own eyes. Hyde trampled a child! He walked over a little girl and never looked back!"

I waved my hand. "Let us talk of

this no more. It was a dark night. Who can say what really happened? Let us just forget the matter."

Utterson shook his head. "I cannot forget it, Henry. I am worried about you. So is Dr. Lanyon. We do not understand why you are friends with such a man."

I put my arm around Utterson.

"Do not worry," I said. "I will tell you something. The moment I wish to, I can make Edward Hyde go away. I give you my word. Now let the matter rest."

"But your new will!" Utterson went on. "This Hyde is going to come into a lot of money if you die. Or . . . disappear. It gives this man every reason to want to be rid of you! It is dangerous, Henry!"

"No, no," I said. "You do not understand. Poor Hyde. He is very young and has much to learn. But I am very close to him, Utterson. So you must promise to do what the will says, if need be."

Utterson sighed. "I still do not like it at all."

Utterson turned to go. Then he

looked back at me. "Perhaps I should meet this new friend of yours, Henry."

"Perhaps," I said. "Your paths may cross one of these days."

"Yes," said Utterson. "I shall see to it that they do." And then he smiled for the first time since he had come into the room. "Yes. If he is Mr. Hyde, why, then, I shall be Mr. Seek!"

Chapter 4

For a while I was a happy man. By day I was a good doctor. I worked long hours helping the sick. But by night I was another man. I did not care who got hurt.

Only one thing bothered me. At

first it had sometimes taken two or even three drinks of my magic drug to change me from Jekyll to Hyde. But after a week or so I did not need so much of the drug to make the change. No. I began to need more of it to change from Hyde *back* to Jekyll! I worried about taking so much of the strong, magic drug. But my life as Hyde was so exciting! I could not give it up.

Nights as Hyde were wild and free! The city of London was mine. I could go anywhere. Do anything. I thought no one would ever guess my secret.

But then one night something happened to change all this. I was just coming back to my laboratory door. I hummed as I turned the key.

"Mr. Hyde, I think?" said a voice.

I gave a low growl. Who would come upon me like this? I turned around and saw Utterson!

Oh, how he hated me! I could see it in his face right away. But he tried not to let his feelings show.

"That is my name," I said. "What do you want?"

"I see that you are going in to see Dr. Jekyll," he said. "I am an old friend of the doctor's. My name is Utterson. I was coming to see him too. Perhaps we can go in together."

My heart beat with fear. What was Utterson doing here? I had to stop him from learning too much.

"Jekyll is not home," I said.

"No?" returned Utterson. "Then I will be going." He bowed. "But it is good that we have met."

"Yes," I said. "We may meet again someday, Utterson. Someday very soon!"

Utterson's face fell. He could no longer hide his feelings! I laughed to myself. Utterson thought that I was talking about Jekyll's will! He thought that I was going to kill Jekyll to get all his money!

Quickly I opened my lab door and went in. Then how I laughed! Poor old Utterson! He was trying to save Jekyll from an evil enemy! Little did he know that he was trying to save Jekyll from himself!

Once inside the lab, I made more of the drug. I swallowed it and felt the sudden breaking of my bones. The hot pain. The shaking. In a matter of seconds I was Henry Jekyll once more.

I went straight up to my bedroom, across the garden. I needed to rest. Then I would begin another day of helping others. As my head touched the pillow, I fell into a deep sleep. I never dreamed of what was to come.

When I woke up the next day, I felt strange. What was wrong? I looked about me. My room was the same. I saw the yellow candle by my bedside. My chair. My brown bedcover that I had slept under for years. Still,

something was out of place. Then my eyes fell upon my hand on the bed-cover. The hand I saw on the bed was small and thick. It was dark and hairy too.

I must have stared at that hand for a full minute before it came to me. It was the hand of Edward Hyde! I jumped from my bed. I rushed to the mirror. My blood turned to ice. I had gone to bed as Henry Jekyll. But I had woken up as Edward Hyde! How had this happened? And what was I to do about it?

Quickly I threw on my robe. I made my way back to the lab. I had to drink more of my magic drug. On the way back across the garden, I saw Poole. He looked surprised to see Hyde at this hour of the day. I gave him a dark grin and went on my way.

Ten minutes later I was sitting at the breakfast table. Once again I was Henry Jekyll. But I must say that morning I did not eat much of my breakfast.

Chapter 5

Waking as Edward Hyde scared me. The change had come without the drug. But how?

I remembered the first time that Edward Hyde had appeared. He was small and weak. But of late he had been growing stronger. Much stronger. Strong enough to get rid of the sleeping Henry Jekyll!

Hyde was growing stronger and more evil. This, too, scared me.

And so I made a promise. No more magic drug. No more Edward Hyde. Ever. I put away Hyde's clothes. I hid the key to his rooms in Soho. From that moment on, I was going to be Henry Jekyll. Only Henry Jekyll.

I kept my promise to live without Hyde. Two months went by. I decided to celebrate living a good life again with a party.

On the night of the party Poole looked very happy.

"I must say, sir," he said. "It is good to have your friends here once again."

"Yes, Poole," I replied. "I have not seen them for a long time."

Poole showed in Utterson, Dr. Lanyon, and several others. We had a pleasant dinner. At one point Lanyon stood up. He raised his glass to me.

"It is good to see you again, Henry," he said. "You have been keeping to yourself for too long."

"True," I said. "I have missed you too. From now on, things will be different."

"Different, eh?" Lanyon went on. "Does that mean you have given up those ideas of yours?" He laughed and turned to Utterson. "Do you remember, Utterson? Henry thought he had discovered a great secret! He thought that he could separate man into two parts! A good part and a bad part!"

"I remember," said Utterson.

I looked long into the fire. At last I looked up at Lanyon.

"Yes, Lanyon," I said. "I have given up those ideas."

Inside I felt angry. My ideas were right. Yet Lanyon was still laughing at me. I had given up being Edward Hyde. But still. I *was* right.

Utterson pulled out his pocket watch. "It's past ten," he said. "I must be going. I have to see our friend Carew. He wants me to draw up some papers for him."

Lanyon stood up. "Well, I must get home, too, Henry. Thank you so much for the fine dinner. We will have to do it again soon. At my house."

I showed the men to the door. I

smiled as I said good-bye. But inside!
Inside I was filled with anger!

No sooner was the door closed than
I turned to Poole.

"I will be working late in my lab
tonight," I told him. "I must be left
alone."

Away I hurried to my lab. My

promise meant nothing to me now.

Do I need to tell you what I did there? How I poured the powder into the red liquid? My hand shook. I was so eager! I had to be careful not to spill it, for I did not have much of the powder left. The red liquid began to boil. When the smoke cleared, I swallowed the drug. I gasped! Henry Jekyll was disappearing. Gone! And there was Edward Hyde!

And what a Hyde! For two months I had kept this evil animal caged inside me. Now he was out! Out with the anger of a hundred howling monsters. I got out Hyde's clothes and threw them on. They were not so loose now. In these two months Hyde had grown bigger. And stronger. I burst out into the quiet London night.

As I raced down the street, I saw someone coming toward me. It was an old man. His white hair looked like a halo in the moonlight. He came closer. And I saw that it was Sir Danvers Carew. Going, I guessed, to meet Utterson.

The old man smiled at me. And then he stopped. I looked into his eyes. Such kind eyes. He asked me directions, smiling as he spoke. Here was a man as good and trusting as a child. His goodness made me even more angry. I don't know why, but it did. As he talked I raised my cane and hit him full in the face. The look in his eyes filled me with a twisted joy! Again I hit him. And again and again. With every blow, I grew more excited. I kept hitting the old man until there

was no life left in him. And even then I did not stop. The thrill of killing had me in its hold.

Then suddenly I heard a loud scream. I looked back at my house. At one of the windows I saw my maid, Amanda. She had been watching! She had seen it all!

"Police!" she cried. "Help! Some-one! Help! A murder! A most terrible murder!"

With one last blow that broke my cane, I left Carew. I looked up at the window again. My maid was still there. Screaming! Lights were going on in other houses. Soon there would be many people on the street.

"There is the killer!" Amanda screamed. "There! Stop him! Stop that man! I know him! It is Edward Hyde!"

Chapter 6

With Amanda's screams still ringing in my ears, I ran away. I did not stop until I was in Soho.

I stayed there all night. No one had heard about the murder yet. What a night I had! Every drink I took, I drank to the dead man's name! What joy I felt to have killed someone.

But at last I went back to Jekyll's house. Oh, so carefully, I crept down the streets near my house and into my lab. Once more I drank the drug. I was Jekyll again. And then all joy was gone. I fell to my knees. Tears ran down my face. Hyde had often hurt others. But this! This was murder. The murder of a good man. How could all my work as Jekyll make up for the evil of Hyde?

I went quickly to my room and fell asleep. I wanted to sleep to forget. But my dreams would not let me. The red blood on my cane. Carew's face. Smashed to bits!

When I woke up, I heard voices outside. I went to the window. There

I saw a boy on the street. He was holding up the newspaper. The headlines were so big that I could read them from my window.

CAREW MURDERED. POLICE LOOK
FOR EDWARD HYDE.

There was a drawing of my face. It took up nearly the whole front page. Amanda must have told what I looked like.

I jumped back from the window. The news was out! The world now knew of Edward Hyde.

But suddenly I felt a great load lift from me. If Hyde showed his face anywhere, he would be handed over to the police. He would be hung by the neck until he was dead! Now there was no choice anymore. If I wanted to stay alive, I had to stay Henry Jekyll. Forever.

"Poole!" I cried out.

"Sir!" answered my butler. He came to my door.

"Poole, please open my office," I said. "I am ready to see patients now."

"Yes, sir," said Poole. Then he added, "Have you heard the terrible news, sir? The news of Sir Danvers Carew?"

"Yes, Poole," I replied. "And of Hyde. I should never have let that man in my house. But you can be sure of one thing. He will never show his face here again."

"No, sir," said Poole. "Many people wish to see him hang for what he did."

"Yes, yes," I said. "Now. Do as I ask you. I wish to help as many people as I can today."

Once again I threw myself into my work. I helped so many people. I did all I could to make up for the evil that Edward Hyde had done in the world. I worked late into the night. Then I dropped off to sleep. I left myself no time for thinking. But was Edward Hyde dead? No! I could feel him within me, trying to get out! I tried my best to keep him quiet.

One day, after I had seen many sick people, I felt the need for some fresh air. I went to a park. It was a fine, clear day. The park was full of birds singing. Spring was in the air. I sat on a bench in the sun. I felt warm and pleasant. My eyes started to close. I remembered a night. A night in Soho.

At that moment I began to shake. I felt sick. I fell off the park bench. When I got up, I felt better. The sick feeling was gone. Then I looked down. The hands that lay on my knees were small and hairy. I was Hyde again!

My heart jumped! I looked around. No one had seen me. Not yet. But on every corner was a newspaper telling what I looked like. It was only a matter of time! I would be caught! And hanged!

I had no idea what to do! I rushed off. Where could I go? If I went back to my house, Poole would call the police. My room in Soho was not safe. I ran through the park, hiding my face.

Just outside the park gate I saw a free carriage. I jumped in. I covered my face so the driver could not see me. My mind raced. I remembered an old hotel on the other side of the city. Maybe I would be safe there.

"Portland Street!" I yelled to the driver. "To the hotel."

The ride was long. I felt safe, hiding inside the carriage. It gave me time to think. I made a plan.

The Portland Street Hotel was as I remembered it. Dark. Out of the way. Inside an old man took me upstairs to a room. A back room. I was safe. But for how long?

I called for paper and pen. Then I wrote two letters.

The first was to Dr. Lanyon. I needed help, but I could not go to Utterson. He had seen Hyde's face. Dr. Lanyon never had. I smiled. Lanyon had laughed at me. Now I could use him to get what I needed.

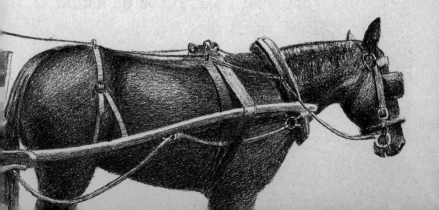

Dear Dr. Lanyon,

My dear old friend! You must help me now. I know we have different ideas. But do not think of that now. My life is in your hands. Please. If you do not help me tonight, I am lost. Please do as I ask.

Tonight, go to my house. Poole will let you in. Go to my lab. There you will see a desk. One of the drawers is marked with an E. In it is some white powder and some red liquid. Take the drawer back to your house.

Wait there until midnight. At that time you will hear a knock on your door. It will be a small man. He will say that he has come from me. Give the drawer to him.

That is all I ask. If you do not do it, I will surely die.

Your friend,
Henry Jekyll

I wrote the whole letter and signed it in Jekyll's writing. Then I wrote another letter to Poole.

Dear Poole,

I am away from home. I will not be back for some time. So I will need your help.

Tonight Dr. Lanyon will come to the door. You are to let him in. Then show him to my laboratory. He is to take a drawer from my desk with him.

Dr. Lanyon is carrying out my orders. Please help him in any way you can.

Thank you,
Henry Jekyll

I sent the letters out by a boy from the hotel. I paid him well to take the letters.

And then I waited. I waited for night to come. I walked up and down that dark little room!

At last a church bell told me it was eleven. I set out for Lanyon's house on foot, under the cover of the dark night.

Chapter 7

As a church bell sounded twelve o'clock, I knocked on Lanyon's door. He opened it. And just in time too. For a policeman was coming down the street. I went quickly inside the house.

"Are you the man Jekyll sent?" Lanyon asked.

"I am," I replied. I had to keep my face in shadow. What if Lanyon had read what Hyde looked like?

I lifted my eyes to look at Lanyon. I could see that he, too, hated me at once.

"Have you got it?" I asked. "The drawer?" I put my hand on Lanyon's arm as if to squeeze the answer out of him.

He stepped back.

"Just a minute," Lanyon said. "You forget. I do not know you. Please. Be seated."

I sat down. I tried to act calm. But I could not.

"I beg you!" I said in a broken whisper. "I am here on an important matter. A matter of life and death. I must not take much time. Henry Jekyll needs this drawer!"

Lanyon looked at me. He could see that I had to have the drawer. And I could see that he wanted to find out what was happening.

"There is the drawer," he said. "On the floor. Behind the table."

I jumped up. I ran to the drawer. My hands were shaking as I looked inside. There! There was all that I needed to save my life! I let out a short cry of joy!

Again I turned to Lanyon. He looked so puzzled.

"Do you have a large glass?" I asked.

He got me one.

I poured in the red liquid. And then

I added the powder. There was only a little of it left now. The mixture in the glass foamed and bubbled. I held it up above my head.

I grinned at Lanyon. "And so," I said. "What is your wish? Shall I take this glass and the drawer and go from your house? Or do you want to know what will happen when I drink this?"

"Drink it?" said Lanyon, surprised. "But what about Jekyll? The things in this drawer are to be taken to him. Are they not?"

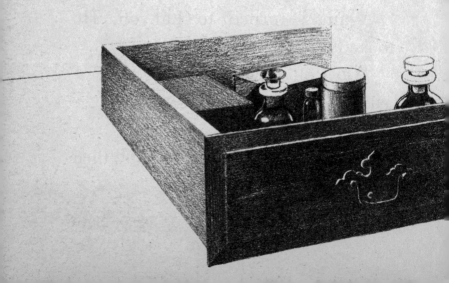

"Jekyll will get what he needs," I said. "Now. Will you have me stay or go? Think before you answer. I will do only what you say. But I warn you. If you watch me drink what is in this glass, you will never be the same. Your eyes shall be opened. Now! Decide!"

"You speak in riddles," said Lanyon. He walked up and down the room for a moment. Then he said, "I suppose I have gone too far with this. I want to know more. Drink! I wish to see this to the end."

"Good!" I cried. "But remember, Lanyon! You are a doctor. You may not tell what you see. It will be our secret! And now! You who have laughed at magic! Look!"

With that I put the glass to my lips. I drank the drug in one gulp. I gave a cry. I began to shake. I held on to the table. But still I fell to the floor. When I got up again, I stood before Lanyon as Henry Jekyll.

"Oh, no!" cried Lanyon. "It cannot be! No! No!"

"Yes, Lanyon," I whispered. "It is. It is."

For the next hour I told Lanyon my story. From beginning to end. I could see that every word of my terrible story seemed to drain a little more life from him. And when I left him that night, he was an old man. Death was written on his face.

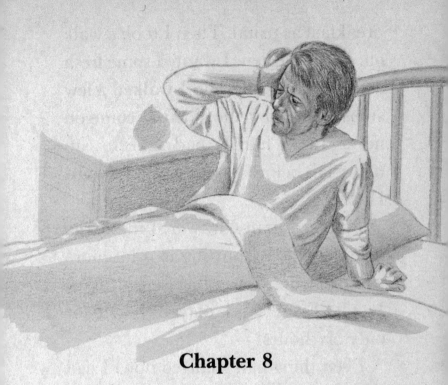

Chapter 8

I walked slowly from Lanyon's house to my own. And then I slept. For how long, I cannot say. But when I woke, I felt so good. To be home. Near my drugs.

That morning Poole made me

breakfast as usual. Then I took a walk out in the garden. I wanted some fresh air. But no sooner had I walked a few steps than I felt the shaking come on me again. I hardly had time to run to my lab before I turned into Edward Hyde!

I dashed to my drawer. I made the drink again. By putting in a lot more white powder, I was able to bring back Jekyll. Even so, I stayed Jekyll for only six hours!

Everything had changed now! I had to keep taking the drug to stay as Henry Jekyll. If I went to sleep, even for a moment, I woke up as Hyde! And Hyde was growing stronger each day. While Jekyll grew sick and weak.

What could I do? I had to stay in my lab. Day and night. Poole brought my food. He would leave it outside the door of my lab. Then, when he was gone, I would open the door. I would take the food and close myself in my lab once more.

I was running out of the powder. I sent notes to Poole under my door. I made him look for more of the white powder in every drugstore in London. But though he brought back large piles of the powder, it was never the same. None of it was like the first powder. None of it worked.

When I was Hyde, I wanted to break out of the lab. It was a cage! A jail! I wanted to be free. But I was so afraid of being seen. I did not want to hang. And so Hyde would always drink the drug that turned him back into Jekyll.

One afternoon I heard something from across the garden.

"Jekyll!" called a voice.

I came to the window in my lab. And saw Utterson. He was walking with his cousin, Enfield.

I tried to smile. "Hello!" I said.

"Hello!" said Utterson. "I hope you are better. I have tried to see you. Many times. But Poole said you were sick. You and Lanyon both. I am worried about the two of you."

"I am not well," I said. "Not well at all." I hung my head, thinking of Lanyon.

"You stay inside too much," said

Utterson. He and Enfield came closer to my window.

"Why don't you come out for a walk with us?" said Enfield.

"Yes!" said Utterson. "Get your hat and cane. Come out now."

"You are very good," I said. "I should like to very much. But no. No, it is out of the question."

I looked at Utterson. He looked back at me with a worried smile. The smile of a true friend.

"Well," said the lawyer, "if you cannot come out, then we must talk from where we are."

"Very well," I said.

A warm feeling came over me. I wanted so to talk with good friends.

"The police are still looking for Carew's murderer, you know," said

Enfield. "They will find him. Sooner or later."

"Yes, Henry," said Utterson. "You are well rid of that young friend of yours. That Mr. Hyde."

"Oh," I replied. "If only I were! If only I were!"

And then the shaking started again! They could see that something horrible was happening to me.

I jumped up! I slammed down the window! Right in their faces! I pulled the curtains closed!

In a moment, as Edward Hyde, I peeked out from behind the curtains. I watched the two men go. I could see the horror in their eyes.

How much had they seen?

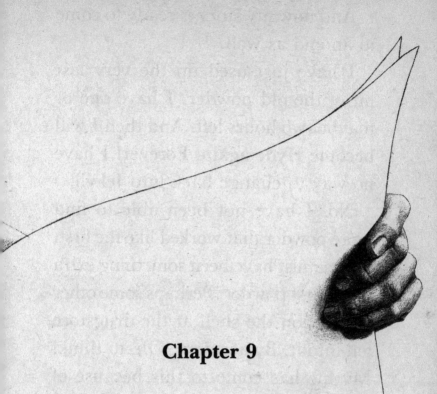

Chapter 9

Dr. Lanyon is dead! I read it in the newspaper that Poole put outside my door this morning. No one knows why he died. Except me. I know. He was scared to death. He was killed by the same man who killed Carew. Me!

And now my story is ready to come to an end as well.

I have just used up the very last bit of the old powder. I have one or maybe two hours left. And then I will become Hyde again. Forever! I have no way to change back into Jekyll.

No, I have not been able to find more powder that worked like the first. There must have been something extra in the first powder. Perhaps some other powder on the shelf at the drugstore fell into it. By accident. Oh, to think! My life has come to this because of some silly accident!

What's that sound? It is Poole knocking on the door. He knows that something is wrong. Very wrong.

"Sir!" he shouts. "I must see you. To make sure that you are well.

I am afraid for your life!"

My trusted Poole. He is afraid for my life!

"Go away!" I cry. "If you want to help me, then leave me alone!"

But what is this? Another voice! It is the voice of Utterson I hear!

"Jekyll!" he cries. "Poole has sent for me. He says that he has not seen you for weeks! He says a strange voice sometimes comes from your lab. He is worried that you are being held there! By Edward Hyde!"

"Go!" I say. "I beg you! Leave me!"

"For your own good, we cannot leave!" answers Utterson. "We are coming in. We are going to break down the door."

I will not answer them. Not anymore. For what is the use? In a short time I will be gone. They will find my writing. That is, if Hyde does not find it first! And they will know my sad, sad story.

But I must keep writing now. For I have one more secret to tell. There is a tall glass on the table beside me. In it is another drug. One that will bring a quick end to whoever drinks it.

Oh! There is the axe breaking down my door! Utterson and Poole are coming. I feel the shaking about to start! Hyde is breaking through too! I am reaching for the glass. There! I have drunk it. This is all. . . . This is the end. The end of Dr. Jekyll *and* Mr. Hyde!

tevenson was born in Scotland in 1850. He was sick most of his life. Because he thought that a change in climate would improve his health, Stevenson traveled a great deal—to Europe, the United States, and the South Seas. But his illnesses did not keep him from his greatest loves—reading and writing. He wrote constantly and became one of the most popular writers of his time.

Stevenson is best known for writing *Kidnapped, Treasure Island,* and *The Strange Case of Dr. Jekyll and Mr. Hyde.* He also wrote *A Child's Garden of Verses,* a collection of poetry for children.

Robert Louis Stevenson died on the South Sea island of Samoa at the age of forty-four.

Kate McMullan has always been intrigued by Robert Louis Stevenson's classic horror story. She has seen nearly all of the ten movie versions of *Dr. Jekyll and Mr. Hyde.* Kate lives in New York City with her husband and daughter.

Paul Van Munching has illustrated covers for several science fiction and fantasy books. For the artwork in *Dr. Jekyll and Mr. Hyde* he worked from photographs to create illustrations that have a highly realistic yet haunting quality. Paul lives in Darien, Connecticut.